This igloo book belongs to:

....

igloobooks

Published in 2016
by Igloo Books Ltd
Cottage Farm
Sywell
NN6 0BJ
www.igloobooks.com

LEO002 0116
2 4 6 8 10 9 7 5 3 1
ISBN 978-1-78557-652-2

Written by Jenny Woods
Illustrated by Richard Watson

Printed and manufactured in China

PIRATE PETE AND HIS PARROT

WRITTEN BY
Jenny Woods

ILLUSTRATED BY
Richard Watson

igloobooks

Once, there was a pirate called Pete who had a purple parrot. Other parrots could say, "Pretty Polly!" and "Pieces of Eight!", but not Pete's.

Pete's parrot could only say one thing.
"He did it!" squawked the silly bird.
It got Pete into all sorts of trouble.

One day, while the pirates were busy cleaning the deck of the Jolly Crossbone, Captain Barnacle strolled past.

SPLOSH!

He didn't see a bucket of soapy water in his way and stepped straight into it.

Suddenly, a voice from the crow's nest shouted, "Land ahoy!" They had arrived at a desert island.

Pete went to pick fruit for his parrot, while the other pirates searched for buried treasure.

The captain was so busy looking at his treasure map, he fell down a great big hole.

"Who dug this hole?" he bellowed, shaking the sand out of his hat.

"He did it!"

Captain Barnacle was so angry, he marched Pete back onto the ship. "Now I need a big drink and a nice snack," he said. He took down his special biscuit barrel from the cabin shelf.

"Aaaargh!" cried the captain, peering inside. "Who's eaten all my best biscuits?"

The purple parrot quickly swallowed the last few crumbs. Then, he landed on Pete's shoulder and squawked,

"He did it!"

Captain Barnacle's face turned red with rage.

He looked at his soggy boot, his sandy hat and his empty biscuit barrel.

"The next time you cross me, you'll be walking the plank!" roared the captain, stomping off.

"It's not fair," grumbled Pete. "I wish I was captain, then I wouldn't get into trouble so much." He picked up the captain's hat and plopped it on his head.

As soon as Pete put on the hat, a black ship sailed alongside the Jolly Crossbone.

A band of nasty pirates was preparing to jump on-board. "Give us all your gold!" they cried, waving their cutlasses in the air.

Suddenly, one of the pirates froze with fear. "Look," he whispered. "That captain looks like Hideous Harry, the world's scariest pirate." He pulled out a poster, which looked just like Pete and his parrot.

"I heard that Hideous Harry caught a giant squid by tying up its tentacles," said one pirate.

Pete's parrot swooped through the air and shrieked loudly,

"He did it!"

"I heard he was a champion sword fighter and won a tournament with an arm tied behind his back!" cried a peg-legged pirate.

"I heard he stole the sea witch's magic wand," added another, "and turned his enemies into jellyfish!"

"Be gone, you bunch of bandits," he bellowed, waving the mop at them, "or I'll turn you all into sea slugs."

"It's the **sea witch's wand**," they whimpered.
"He really **IS** Hideous Harry!"

"Help!" screamed the nasty pirates.
"Run away!" Pushing and shoving each other,
they scrambled back to their own ship.

The black ship speedily set sail, leaving
a trail of white foam frothing along
behind it.

Pete took off the captain's hat and put it back on the ship's wheel.
With a flap of his purple wings, the parrot landed on Pete's shoulder.
"Maybe you aren't such a bad pet after all," smiled Pete.

Captain Barnacle climbed out of his cabin just in time to see the ship disappear over the horizon. "Well done, me hearty," he said to Pete. "You deserve a reward for being so brave."

He gave Pete a bulging bag of gold coins and the purple parrot an even bigger bag of birdseed. "Who saved the Jolly Crossbone from a band of fearsome pirates?" asked Captain Barnacle.